S0-AZO-680

LET YOUR IMAGINATION TAKE FLIGHT

FOR TOM SGOUROS

No part of this publication may be reproduced in whole or in part,
or stored in a retrieval system, or transmitted in any form or by
any means, electronic, mechanical, photocopying, recording,
or otherwise, without written permission of the publisher.
For information regarding permission, write to Permissions,
Houghton Mifflin Company, 215 Park Avenue South,
New York, NY 10003.

ISBN 0-590-70632-2

Copyright © 1991 by David Wiesner.
All rights reserved. Published by Scholastic Inc.,
555 Broadway, New York, NY 10012, by arrangement with
Houghton Mifflin Company.

SCHOLASTIC and associated logos are trademarks and/or
registered trademarks of Scholastic Inc.

12 11 10 9 8 7 6 5 4 3   0 1 2 3/0

Printed in the U.S.A.   08

First Scholastic paperback printing, September 1998

Illustrations executed in watercolor on Arches paper.

The type is Bulmer.

TUESDAY

DAVID WIESNER

SCHOLASTIC INC.

New York Toronto London Auckland Sydney
Mexico City New Delhi Hong Kong

TUESDAY EVENING, AROUND EIGHT.

11:21 P.M.

4:38 A.M.

NEXT TUESDAY, 7:58 P.M.